DATE DUE			
MAR 1 8 2002			

462    $15.95

GIF   Giff, Patricia   992281
                       Reilly.

                       Say hola, Sarah

Say Hola, Sarah

Say Hola, Sarah

2
Friends and Amigos

BY PATRICIA REILLY GIFF

Illustrated by DyAnne DiSalvo-Ryan

Gareth Stevens Publishing
MILWAUKEE

For a free color catalog describing Gareth Stevens' list of high-quality
books and multimedia programs, call 1-800-542-2595 (USA) or
1-800-461-9120 (Canada).
Gareth Stevens Publishing's Fax: (414) 225-0377.
See our catalog, too, on the World Wide Web: http://gsinc.com

Library of Congress Cataloging-in-Publication Data

Giff, Patricia Reilly.
    Say hola, Sarah / by Patricia Reilly Giff ; illustrated by
DyAnne DiSalvo-Ryan.
        p. cm. — (Friends and amigos)
    Summary: Sarah is too embarrassed to speak Spanish in front of her
friends at the Columbus Day party until Anna's cousin from Colombia
explains her own secret fear.
    ISBN 0-8368-2050-9 (lib. bdg.)
    [1. Spanish language—Fiction. 2. Columbus Day—Fiction.
3. Friendship—Fiction.] I. DiSalvo-Ryan, DyAnne, ill. II. Title.
III. Series: Giff, Patricia Reilly. Friends and amigos.
PZ7.G3626Sb 1998
[Fic]—dc21   97-40657

This edition first published in 1998 by
Gareth Stevens Publishing
1555 North RiverCenter Drive, Suite 201
Milwaukee, Wisconsin 53212 USA

Text © 1995 by Patricia Reilly Giff. Illustrations © 1995 by DyAnne DiSalvo-Ryan.
Published by arrangement with Bantam Doubleday Dell Books for Young Readers,
a division of Bantam Doubleday Dell Publishing Group, Inc., New York, New York.
All rights reserved. Additional end matter © 1998 by Gareth Stevens, Inc.

Printed in the United States of America

1 2 3 4 5 6 7 8 9 02 01 00 99 98

For Alice, the October bride,
with love

Where to find the Spanish Lessons in this book:

Say Hola, Sarah

SARAH'S SPANISH NOTEBOOK

Saludos *(sah-LOO-dohs)*	Greetings
Hola! *(OH-lah)*	Hi!
¿Qué tal? *(keh TAHL)*	What's up?
¿Cómo te llamas? *(KOH-moh teh YAH-mahs?)*	What's your name?
Me llamo Anna. *(meh YAH-moh AH-nah)*	My name is Anna.
¿Cómo estás? *(KOH-moh es-TAHS?)*	How are you?
¡Muy bien! *(MOOEE beeEHN)*	Just fine!

1

"Three o'clock," said Mrs. Halfpenny.

Sarah Cole slammed her book shut.

She raced to the closet for her jacket.

She was out the classroom door in two seconds . . . right behind her best friend, Anna.

She slid to a stop. "Wait. I forgot my Christopher Columbus book."

She went back to grab the book out of her desk. She caught up with Anna at the corner.

"No more pencils, no more books," Anna was saying.

Sarah held out her arms. "No school for three days."

"And a surprise at the library," said Anna. "All because of Christopher Columbus."

Sarah shuffled through the leaves at the curb. She didn't want to think about Christopher Columbus. She didn't want to think about the mess Benjamin Bean had gotten her into.

Someone jumped into the leaves in back of her.

Benjamin, of course.

"*¡Caramba!*" said Sarah.

"Don't pay attention to him," said Anna.

Sarah made believe she didn't see him.

"I'm going to tell you a pack of Spanish words for your notebook," Anna said.

Sarah nodded. She was learning Spanish . . . trying to learn Spanish. Anna spoke it every day at home. Lucky Anna!

"Now, listen," Anna said. *"Me llamo Anna.* It sounds like meh YAH-moh."

Sarah nodded. *"Me llamo Anna."*

Anna laughed. "No. Your name is Sarah."

Behind them Benjamin was shouting. *"Me llamo* the *Niña,* the *Pinta,* the *Santa María."*

He laughed. "I mean the *Sarah María."*

"Close your mouth, Benjamin," Anna said. *"Por favor."*

Benjamin stuck his nose up next to Sarah's. "Get it? Christopher Columbus's ships? The *Niña . . ."*

Sarah stepped back.

Benjamin had tomato sauce on one cheek. A piece of spaghetti was stuck to his shirt. Something blue was under his nails.

Something blue?

Sarah tried to think. Yes. Blueberry muffins for school lunch dessert.

"*¡Qué desastre!*" Anna said in Spanish.

"*¡Qué desastre!*" Sarah repeated. Anna had taught her that yesterday. *Awful.* That was Benjamin . . . sometimes.

He darted away from them. He twirled around the telephone pole.

Then he started up Higby Avenue, running backward, making faces all the way.

"*Desastre,*" Anna said again. "I'm glad we won't see him again for three days."

Sarah took a deep breath. "But . . ."

"Now Spanish," Anna said. "*¿Cómo estás?*"

"What does that mean again?" Sarah asked.

Before Anna could answer, Benjamin stopped at the corner. "Don't forget," he called. "We have to do the Christopher Columbus story for the class on Tuesday."

Sarah closed her eyes.

That Benjamin.

He had told Mrs. Halfpenny he wanted to do a Christopher Columbus story.

"Sarah will do it with me," he had said.

Before she had opened her mouth, he had waved his arm around. "We'll do it for the whole class," he had said.

"Terrible," Sarah said right now. She hoped Tuesday would never come.

"It's the same in Spanish, teh-RREE-bleh," Anna said. *"Terrible."*

Sarah watched Benjamin turn the corner.

Terrible was right.

SARAH'S SPANISH NOTEBOOK

Buenos modales (booEH-nohs moh-DAH-lehs)	**Good Manners**
Por favor. (pohr fah-VOR)	Please.
Gracias. (GRAH-seeahs)	Thank you.
De nada. (deh NAH-dah)	You're welcome.
Perdóname. (pehr-DOH-nah-meh)	Excuse me.
Lo siento. (loh seeEHN-toh)	I'm sorry.

2

Sarah opened the back door. "Don't you love Friday?" she asked Aunt Minna, the baby-sitter.

Aunt Minna had breadsticks and apple slices on the kitchen table. "Sarah," she said. "I love you kids messing up the whole place all weekend."

Sarah laughed. She loved Aunt Minna.

Aunt Minna was as skinny as the breadsticks. Her hair was tied up in a tiny ball on top of her head.

Sarah sat for a while. Then she went upstairs.

She had to look perfect for the library surprise.

She pulled everything out of the closet until she found her yellow shirt that said VÁMONOS. Anna had told her it meant "Let's go."

Downstairs, Aunt Minna called up, "Anna's here."

Sarah pulled on the shirt. She opened her bottom drawer. She reached for her mother's old lipstick.

Her little sister, Erica, had been there first.

She had knocked the top off.

The lipstick was in a big glob.

Sarah shook her head. She rubbed on a tiny smear with her fingers.

She smacked her lips together.

Then she raced down the stairs.

Anna looked different from an hour ago.

She had cut bangs across her forehead. They were long and crooked and almost covered her eyes.

"Nice," said Sarah.

Anna pushed up her bangs to see. "I wanted to try something new." She smiled. *"Muchas gracias."*

Sarah tried to think. *"Lo siento."*

Anna frowned a little.

Erica stuck her head out from the kitchen.

Lipstick was all over her mouth.

"That's 'I'm sorry,'" she said. "You mean *De nada.*"

Sarah felt her face get hot.

Erica danced around them. "I'll come with you."

Sarah sighed. "I don't think . . ."

Aunt Minna came down the hall. "What about all those papers on the kitchen floor?" she asked Erica. "Bits and pieces, and scissors, and crayons, and . . ."

"Don't worry," Erica said. "I'm making a nice scrapbook. It's for you."

Aunt Minna rolled her eyes. "I'll help." She winked at Sarah and Anna.

Sarah went out the door ahead of Anna.

They hurried down the street and rounded the corner.

Sarah grinned at Anna. "Aunt Minna just saved our lives."

In front of them was the sound of branches cracking.

Benjamin swung out of the tree. "*Hasta la vista,*" he said.

He followed them all the way to the library. Sarah tried not to pay attention to him.

She was telling Anna all the Spanish she knew. *"Uno, dos, tres . . .* One, two, three . . ."

They opened the library door. On it was a sign.

A SURPRISE
AT
SPRINGFIELD
GARDENS
PUBLIC LIBRARY
TO CELEBRATE

◊ CHRISTOPHER ◊
COLUMBUS

STOP IN.
FIND OUT ABOUT IT.

Inside, kids were all over the place.
So was a pile of Spanish books.
Another sign was taped to the wall.

MONDAY IS COLUMBUS DAY.
JOIN THE FUN.
COLUMBUS DAY CAKE.
SANTA MARÍA SODA.
PICK A PARTNER.
TALK IN SPANISH.

Everyone was excited. No wonder, Sarah thought. Everyone was dying to speak Spanish.

Benjamin leaned over Mrs. Muñoz's desk. "Christopher Columbus didn't even come from Spain," he said.

Mrs. Muñoz smiled. "You're right, Benjamin. But Queen Isabella of Spain sent him across the ocean . . ."

Benjamin grinned at Sarah. "On the *Niña*, the . . ."

Anna looked up. "My mother didn't come from Spain, either. She speaks Spanish, though."

"Many people speak Spanish," said Mrs. Muñoz. "From Mexico, from Chile, from Colombia, from Ecuador . . ."

"That's where my mother is from." Anna tapped Sarah's arm. "Let's sign up."

Sarah nodded. She loved the sound of Spanish. If only she knew more words.

Anna was waiting . . . smiling.

Sarah signed her name. She followed Anna out the door.

"This is easy," Anna said. "We'll be partners. You'll study your notebook."

Benjamin jumped down the steps. "I'll be someone's partner."

"No, thanks." Anna looked at Sarah. "We'll talk with each other . . ."

Sarah swallowed. She had to learn Spanish in just three days.

3

It was Saturday morning.

Sarah was sitting with her back against the big rock in the woods.

It wasn't a real woods. It was the space between her house and Anna's.

It was filled with sticker bushes and weeds, and a couple of trees. Right now Sarah's father was standing at one end.

He was painting a picture of the leaves.

They didn't look like leaves. They looked like red dots and yellow squares.

Sarah was talking to herself.

She was talking quietly.

The woods weren't that big.

She looked down at her notebook. "*¿Cómo estás?*" she whispered to herself.

She squinched up her eyes. She tried not to look at the answer.

In her mind, she could hear Anna saying, "All we have to do is talk back and forth, talk about anything. The audience will listen . . ."

"*¿Cómo estás? . . .*" Sarah's hands felt wet. An audience. She loved Spanish. What she didn't love was saying it in front of the whole world.

"*Hola.*" Benjamin Bean poked his head out from behind a juniper bush.

Sarah closed her eyes. "Go away, Benjamin."

"What about our Christopher Columbus story?" he asked.

She opened her eyes. "Why are you wearing that red winter hat? Are you crazy?"

Benjamin climbed up on the top of the rock. "I knew it," he said. "You don't know one thing about Christopher."

"I do so," she began.

She could hear someone coming.

Erica. And Thomas Attonichi.

"Give me some peace," she said.

That's what Aunt Minna said every two minutes.

"Good news," said Erica.

"If you'd like to know," Benjamin began at the same time, "Christopher Columbus wore a hat just like this."

"With stains all over it?" Erica asked.

Benjamin jumped off the rock. "Almost everyone thought the world was flat until Columbus came along," he said.

Sarah tried not to pay attention. "¿*Cómo* . . ."

Erica sat down. "¿*Cómo estás?* That means 'How are you?' " She patted Sarah's cheek. "I'm fine," she said. *"Muy bien. Want to hear the news?"*

Sarah put down Mrs. Muñoz's papers.

"Thomas and me are partners," Erica said. "We're going to speak Spanish together at the library."

Sarah looked at Thomas.

He was lying on the ground, half buried in the leaves.

He was blowing bubbles with the piece of bubble gum in his mouth.

"Are you sure he can do it?" Sarah asked.

Thomas didn't talk at all, she thought. She had never heard him say one word.

"Watch," said Erica.

Benjamin held his hands to his eyes like a

telescope. "Look, men," he shouted. "I see land."

Erica leaned over. *"Por favor,* Thomas."

Thomas reached into his pocket.

He pulled out a stick of gum.

"See, Thomas speaks Spanish," Erica said. "I told you so."

Someone was yelling. Screaming. "Saaaa-rrrrrrrah!"

Sarah looked up.

Anna was standing on her back steps. "Wait till you see who's here!" she yelled.

Sarah could see someone else on Anna's steps.

Erica was looking too. "It's Luisa," she said. "Luisa from Colombia."

SARAH'S SPANISH NOTEBOOK

Vístete (VEES-teh-teh)	**Get Dressed**
calcetines (kahl-seh-TEEN-ehs)	socks
camisa (kah-MEE-sah)	shirt
camiseta (kah-mee-SEH-tah)	T-shirt
pantalones (pan-tah-LOHN-ehs)	pants
sombrero (som-BREH-roh)	hat
zapatos (sah-PAH-tohs)	shoes
falda (FAHL-dah)	skirt
chaqueta (chah-KEH-tah)	jacket
¿Qué llevas? (keh YEH-vahs?)	What are you wearing?
Me gusta el color de . . . (meh GOOS-tah el koh-LOHR deh)	I like the color of . . .

4

Sarah stood up slowly.

She dusted off her sweatpants.

Benjamin was standing on tiptoes. "I remember Luisa," he said. "She was always laughing."

Sarah remembered Luisa, too.

Benjamin was right.

Luisa never stopped laughing.

She never stopped talking, either . . . to Anna, in Spanish.

Sarah couldn't understand one word she said.

Sarah climbed over the rock. She started toward Anna's house.

Behind her, Erica was saying, *"Gracias* for the gum, Thomas."

And Benjamin was yelling, "I knew the world was round, men. I knew we wouldn't fall off the edge."

Anna was waving at her. So was Luisa.

Luisa was wearing a sweater with ribbons, and bows in her hair, and fourteen bracelets, and socks with lace.

Everything was pink, even her earrings. They looked like pink diamonds.

Sarah's sweatpants were old. She remembered they were ripped somewhere.

"Hola, Sarah," Luisa called. *"¿Cómo estás? Me gusta el color de tus pantalones."*

Sarah wondered what Luisa was saying. *Pantalones.* Pants? Maybe Luisa had seen the rip.

Anna was smiling and nodding.

At least Sarah could tell them hello.

"OOla," she said.

Luisa began to laugh.

Anna laughed, too.

"Ho-la," they said almost together. "It sounds like 'OH-la.' "

Anna's mother poked her head out the back door. "Time to eat," she said.

"Yes," said Luisa. "Come. Eat the kitchen."

Anna began to laugh. "We could eat the stove and the refrigerator."

Luisa laughed, too. "Wrong?" she asked. "I said it wrong? *¡Caramba!*"

Sarah could hear Erica. "Say 'You're welcome,' Thomas. *'De nada.'* "

She sounded like Sarah's teacher, Mrs. Halfpenny.

And Anna was talking, too. Telling her

that Luisa was going to stay for three days.

Anna's mother smiled. "Come in, Sarah. Have lunch."

Sarah sat down at the table. Then Luisa began again. She spoke so fast, Sarah couldn't tell one word from another.

Was she saying something about her, Sarah wondered? Something about her pants?

Sarah shook her head. "I think Aunt Minna is calling me."

She wished she knew how big the rip was.

Luisa was talking again. "*¿Algo de comer? ¿Algo de beber?*"

And even Anna. "*Plátanos y leche, ¡delicioso!*"

Talking in Spanish a mile a minute.

Sarah wished she could say more than four words.

She got up and started to back away. "Benjamin is waiting. We have to do the Christopher Columbus story."

She took two more steps. Then she started to run.

SARAH'S SPANISH NOTEBOOK

Algo de comer (AHL-go deh coh-MEHR)	Something to Eat
comida (koh-MEE-dah)	food
hamburguesa (ahm-boohr-GEH-sah)	hamburger
papas fritas (PAH-pahs FREE-tahs)	french fries
perro caliente (PEH-rroh kah-leeEHN-teh)	hot dog
ensalada (ehn-sah-LAH-dah)	salad
frutas (FROO-tahs)	fruit
plátanos (PLAH-tah-nohs)	bananas
helado (eh-LAH-doh)	ice cream
torta (TOHR-tah)	cake
dulces (DOOL-sehs)	sweets
¡Delicioso! (deh-lee-seeOH-soh)	Delicious!

5

Sarah sat on the kitchen floor.

Her yellow dog, Gus, was there, too.

He was pulling on her sneaker laces.

"A jar of pickles," said Aunt Minna. "A head of cabbage."

"Not corned beef for supper," Sarah said. "It makes me gag every time."

"I love corned beef," Erica said. She must have gotten into the lipstick again.

It was all over her teeth.

Aunt Minna gave Sarah the money. "Take Erica with you."

"I can go faster alone."

"I'll fly." Erica put her arms out. She made a buzzing noise.

Sarah began to shake her head.

"You won't be able to carry everything," Aunt Minna said. "I need bread from your mother's bakery, and . . ."

"Dessert," said Erica.

"Right," said Aunt Minna.

"Eclairs," said Erica. *"Fantástico."*

"I hate the insides of éclairs," Sarah said.

She felt mean inside, miserable.

Anna and Luisa were over there talking Spanish . . . laughing.

Even Erica spoke Spanish better than she did. If she heard a word once, she remembered it forever.

"We could get Danish," Erica said. *"Delicioso."*

Aunt Minna patted Sarah's head. She put her hand on Sarah's chin.

She didn't say anything.

That was the nicest thing about Aunt Minna, Sarah thought.

She always knew when you were sad.

She didn't ask about it, though.

"Why don't you wait and see about dessert when you get to the bakery," Aunt Minna said.

"We could do that," Erica said. She put her arm through Sarah's. "Come on."

Sarah nodded a little.

They started down the block.

Thomas Attonichi was walking along his driveway.

He was holding out an orange ice cream pop.

It was dripping along the walk.

A row of ants was following him up the path.

"*El helado,*" Erica called.

"Ice cream," she whispered to Sarah. "I think Thomas is working on his Spanish words."

Sarah had to smile. "I think he's feeding the ants."

They turned in at the alley and opened the back door of the bakery.

Inside, everything smelled of bread.

Flour was all over the floor and the tables.

Mannie, the baker, was covered with it.

Even his hair was white.

He smiled when he saw them. "*¿Cómo está tu español?* How is your Spanish?" he asked.

Sarah opened her mouth. *"Muy . . ."*

She tried to think. *Muy* something . . . but what?

Erica knew it already. *"Muy bien,"* she said. "Fine."

Sarah went out in front.

Her mother was helping a woman with ladyfingers.

"Tons of them," said the woman. "I'm having a Columbus Day party."

Columbus Day.

Sarah still hadn't started the story with Benjamin.

She reached for a cookie.

It was a little pink heart.

She thought of Luisa. And Anna.

Luisa would be here for the library party.

How she'd laugh when she heard Sarah trying to speak.

Sarah swallowed.

Anna probably wanted to be partners with Luisa.

"*La galleta*," Erica said in back of her.

Sarah didn't know what that meant. She didn't care, either.

She banged out through the front door. "Come on," she said. "We have to get the cabbage."

SARAH'S SPANISH NOTEBOOK

Algo de beber (AHL-goh deh beh-BEHR)	**Something to Drink**
¡Tengo sed! (TEHN-goh SEHD)	I'm thirsty!
bebida (beh-BEE-dah)	beverage
jugo (HOO-goh)	juice
soda (SOH-dah)	soda or pop
leche (LEH-cheh)	milk
té (TEH)	tea
agua (AH-gwah)	water

It was Sunday.

Sarah picked up her pad and pencil.

She had to find Benjamin.

They had to do that Christopher Columbus story.

Benjamin lived in the apartment house on Higby Avenue.

It was a great place.

You could take the elevator to the second floor . . . or you could hang on the bars, climb the fire escape, and slide in the window.

That's what Benjamin always did.

Right now Sarah went into the lobby.

She pushed the elevator button.

She heard a pounding sound.

It was Benjamin, coming down the stairs.

He blinked when he saw her. *"Hola,"* he said.

"Hola," she said back.

"¿Qué . . ."

She held up her hand. "Talk in English."

He slid down on the floor. He snapped the Velcro on his sneaker. "What are you doing in here, anyway?"

"Christopher . . . ," she began.

He jumped up. He looked out the door. "It's San Salvador."

"What?" she asked.

"That's where he landed," Benjamin said. "In San Salvador. He was looking for someplace else."

41

They went outside to sit on the steps.

"You want me to write?" he asked. "Or do you . . ."

She smoothed out her paper.

She looked at his hands.

Filthy.

"I'd better," she began.

"All right," he said. "Write this. 'Christopher told Queen Isabella to give him a couple of ships.' "

Sarah began in her best handwriting. She didn't know how to spell *Isabella*. She didn't know how to spell *couple*, either.

Just then she saw Anna and Luisa.

They were walking up the street together.

Luisa was waving her arms around.

They were talking in Spanish.

They looked like best friends.

Sarah could never speak Spanish like that.

Not in a hundred years.

If she could look into Anna's head, she knew what she'd see. Anna liking Luisa better than Sarah. Much better. Anna wishing that Luisa was her partner.

They were in front of the steps now . . . still talking, still laughing.

Sarah stood up.

Before she had time to think, she took a step toward them.

"Anna," she called.

Anna pushed up her bangs to see. *"Hola,* Sarah," she said.

Sarah didn't look at her.

She looked at Luisa's pink sneakers. "I can't be your partner for the Columbus party," Sarah said.

Anna was shaking her head. "But why . . ."

Sarah took a breath.

Benjamin slid down the steps toward them. "She's going to be my partner," he said.

Anna stared at them for a moment. "Come on, Luisa," she said.

Sarah looked after them until they turned the corner.

"Why did you say that?" she asked Benjamin. "How could you say that?"

"I don't know." Benjamin raised his shoulders in the air.

"And how could you tell Mrs. Halfpenny I'd do that Christopher Columbus story with you?"

"I guess because you were my friend," Benjamin said.

"I'm not going to be your partner," Sarah said. "I'm not going to be your friend. And I'm not even going to the Columbus Day party."

SARAH'S SPANISH NOTEBOOK

La familia
(lah fah-MEE-leeah)

The Family

---

mi madre
(mee MAH-dreh)

my mother

mi padre
(mee PAH-dreh)

my father

mi hermana
(mee ehr-MAHN-ah)

my sister

mi hermano
(mee ehr-MAHN-oh)

my brother

mi amigo
(mee ah-MEE-goh)

my friend (a boy)

mi amiga
(mee ah-MEE-gah)

my friend (a girl)

mi tía
(mee TEE-ah)

my aunt

7

Sarah opened the kitchen door.

Aunt Minna was punching down yeast dough on a white cloth.

"There's nothing to do," Sarah said.

"Why not go over to your mother's bakery?" Aunt Minna said.

But the bakery was terrible on a Sunday.

A million people in line.

Her mother rushing back and forth.

A skillion honey buns. And Sarah couldn't even taste one crumb. "We need to sell every single one," her mother would say.

Sarah dug her nail into a tiny edge of dough. She made an X.

Her father came into the kitchen.

He had a small paintbrush in his hand. "Come with me."

Sarah thought about it. She couldn't make up her mind.

She didn't have to.

Aunt Minna handed her a bag. "Enough lunch for both of you."

Her father led the way.

Three blocks to Higby Avenue and the railroad station.

He set everything up at the end of the platform. His paints and his easel.

Sarah sat down on a bench to watch.

She looked at the tracks. Two silver ribbons that stretched out forever.

She shaded her eyes to look for a train.

"Perfect," said her father.

He put a squirt of blue on his brush.

Blue for her jeans.

Her father's pictures never looked like real life.

They looked like dots, and streaks, and blobs of paint.

"It's a different way of looking at things," he said.

Sarah squinched up her eyes.

She tried to look at the tracks in a different way.

"You must be excited about the library party," he said.

A train was coming. A black blob of a train.

It never stopped. It whooshed through the station.

Sarah didn't answer.

Her father couldn't hear over the noise, anyway.

After a while she got tired of sitting.

Her father gave her paper and paint of her own.

Sarah painted a pale green box for the library.

She drew Benjamin sitting on the step.

He looked like a squiggle of blue toothpaste.

Too bad for Benjamin.

She put Anna in red—*rojo*.

Anna loved red.

And a pink Luisa. *Rosado.*

Sarah's eyes felt teary.

She put herself in, too, in a corner, outside the library, alone.

A green Sarah—*verde.*

She almost looked like a tree.

A moment later, her father was standing next to her.

She blinked fast.

"I like your painting." He patted her arm. "It looks happy with all those colors. I think it's a picnic."

Sarah nodded a little. "I guess so."

He stepped back. "Maybe it's the park, with flowers and trees. It's happy with all those colors."

She tried to smile.

She didn't want him to know it was the saddest picture she had ever done.

Her father went back to his own painting.

Sarah picked up her brush.

She put an X over the green tree.

She looked at the squiggle that was Benjamin.

She put an X over him, too.

SARAH'S SPANISH NOTEBOOK

| **Quiero . . .** | **I want . . .** |
| (keeEH-roh) | |

Quiero hablar español (keeEH-roh ah-BLAHR eh-spah-NYOHL)	I want to speak Spanish.
Necesito . . . (neh-seh-SEE-toh)	I need . . .
Necesito una amiga. (neh-seh-SEE-toh oo-nah ah-MEE-gah)	I need a friend.

It was almost dinnertime.

Sarah had spent the afternoon trying to write a Christopher Columbus story.

Let Benjamin do one by himself.

How was she going to get up and talk in front of the class, though? All by herself?

Benjamin had been right.

Christopher had worn a red hat.

She had read it in her book.

Christopher's hair had been red, too.

Rojo. Red in Spanish.

She kept thinking about Benjamin . . . Benjamin saying she was his friend.

She had never thought of that.

She looked out her bedroom window.

The last few leaves were drifting off the trees.

The little woods between her house and Anna's didn't look like woods anymore.

Sarah could see all of Anna's house. *La casa de Anna.*

Too bad she was so terrible at Spanish. She loved the sound of it.

Maybe she wouldn't try anymore.

She and Anna might not be friends anymore, either.

Sarah shivered. It was getting dark early, and chilly.

She reached up to close the window.

Someone was in the little woods.

She leaned forward.

Anna?

No. It was Luisa.

She could hear Erica coming down the hall. She was humming Anna's Spanish song. *"Dos y dos . . ."*

What was Luisa doing out there, anyway?

Erica came into the bedroom.

She leaned over Sarah's shoulder. "Luisa is still there," she said.

"What do you mean?" Sarah asked. "Still there?"

"She told me, *'Vete.'* Go away. She was crying."

Sarah leaned against the window. She tried to see.

It did look as if Luisa was crying.

Sarah pulled on her jacket. "I think I'll just see what's happening."

She went outside, through the yard, and into the woods.

Luisa was sitting on the big rock.

Her face was red. She was talking to herself.

"*Hola,*" said Sarah.

"*Hola,*" said Luisa.

"What's the matter?" asked Sarah.

"*Nada.*" Luisa waved her hand. "Speak in Spanish."

Sarah shook her head. "No, in English."

"Too hard for me," Luisa said. "I say it wrong. Everything. Everyone laughs."

"Me too, when I try to speak Spanish," Sarah said slowly.

Luisa made a face. "I have to think every year."

Sarah smiled. "You mean every minute." She boosted herself up on the rock.

She couldn't believe it.

Luisa was having as much trouble as she was.

Sarah thought of her father. Seeing things in a different way.

Then she thought of Benjamin . . . a blue squiggle of toothpaste in her painting.

Benjamin, who wanted to be her friend.

"*Amigas,*" she told Luisa. "We'll help each other."

Luisa was watching her. "*¿Sí?*"

She probably didn't understand one word Sarah was saying.

But that was all right.

Sarah slid off the rock. "Come on, Luisa. I have to tell Benjamin something."

"*Vámonos,*" said Luisa.

Sarah smiled. "I know that word. Let's go."

SARAH'S SPANISH NOTEBOOK

Los días de fiesta *(lohs DEE-ahs deh feeEHS-tah)*	Holidays
Año Nuevo *(AH-nyoh nooEH-voh)*	New Year's
Pascua *(PAH-skwah)*	Easter
La víspera del día de todos los santos *(lah VEE-speh-rah dehl DEE-ah deh TOH-dohs lohs SAHN-tohs)*	Halloween
El Día de la Raza *(ehl DEE-ah deh lah RAH-sah)*	Columbus Day
Acción de Gracias *(ahk-seeOHN deh GRAH- seeahs)*	Thanksgiving
Navidad *(nah-vee-DAHD)*	Christmas
El día de san Valentín *(el DEE-ah deh sahn vah-lehn-TEEN)*	Valentine's Day
El Día de la Independencia *(el DEE-ah deh lah een-deh-pen-DEN-seeah)*	Independence Day

The library was packed. Everyone was speaking Spanish.

Some knew a lot.

Some knew a little.

They all knew more than she did, Sarah thought.

But then she looked at Luisa.

Luisa's eyes were closed.

She was trying to remember words in English.

Sarah looked at the cake on her plate.

Columbus Day cake.

It was shaped like a ship.

The *Niña*, maybe.

She took a tiny bite.

Then she counted.

Anna and Luisa were going to speak next.

Then Erica and Thomas.

Soon it would be her turn.

Hers and Benjamin's.

Anna and Luisa stood in front.

They looked at each other and smiled.

Then they began to talk.

Anna spoke in Spanish.

Luisa spoke in English.

"*Sarah es mi amiga*," said Anna.

"My new friend is Sarah," said Luisa. "She thinks Spanish is hard. I think English is hard."

Then Erica pulled Thomas up to the front. "*Vamos*," she told him.

Thomas was dressed up for the party.

He was wearing a red plaid shirt and a green plaid tie. His hair was slicked back.

He was looking down at the floor.

Erica waited for a moment. Then she whispered to him. "Want me to talk, Thomas?"

She looked at everyone. "He wants me to talk."

She laughed a little. "What we want to say is, *'Feliz Día de la Raza.'* Happy Columbus Day."

"Smile, Thomas," she whispered.

Erica waited another half minute. "That's all."

At last it was Sarah's turn.

She swallowed.

Anna and Luisa were nodding. She and Benjamin had practiced with them. They were lots of help.

"You begin," she told Benjamin.

He nodded. *"Me llamo Cristóbal Colón. Christopher Columbus."*

Sarah took a breath. *"Soy la reina Isabel.* Queen Isabella."

"Ah," said Mrs. Muñoz. *"¡Muy bien!"*

Then Benjamin spoke again. *"Necesito tres . . ."*

"Ships," said Luisa.

"Sí," said Sarah. *"Y algo de comer. Y algo de beber."*

Benjamin thought for a moment. *"Vámonos!"*

Now Luisa spoke.

"He came to a new world, America!"

Everyone clapped.

Benjamin's idea to do the Christopher Columbus story in Spanish had been great.

Luisa handed her a piece of cake.

Sarah sat back.

Spanish wasn't so hard.

Maybe she'd write to Luisa when she went home next week.

And the Christopher Columbus story. It would be simple to do it in English tomorrow! She and Benjamin might even do it again for the class in Spanish.

Anna came to sit next to her.

Sarah opened her mouth to take a bite of cake.

She looked at Anna and smiled. "*¡Deliciosa!*"

LETTER TO LIBRARIANS, TEACHERS, AND PARENTS

Learning a new language can be intimidating. *Friends and Amigos* introduces a basic Spanish vocabulary in a challenging, yet familiar setting. New words are interspersed throughout each chapter and can be assimilated easily and naturally as young readers enjoy the story. The reinforcement that is so important in developing language skills is encouraged at the end of each chapter, where a list of words introduced in the previous pages offers pronunciation guides and basic definitions. *Friends and Amigos* also offers real-life stories that center around bilingual friendships, thus encouraging readers to recognize the tremendous value of cultural diversity in the world community.

The intriguing activities on page 69 help learning take place while having fun. Parents and teachers can incorporate many of these activities on a daily basis. The recommended books, videos, and web sites that follow on page 70 also help provide an enjoyable pathway to learning more about Spanish language and culture. These positive experiences will encourage young readers to explore a language other than their own.

ACTIVITIES

Who is Columbus? Visit a library and find some books about Christopher Columbus. In what country was he born? Why did he want to sail across the Atlantic Ocean? Learn the names of those who financed his voyage. What did he promise in return? Describe what Columbus found after he crossed the ocean. Did he make other voyages? How rich did his discoveries make him? What happened to him near the end of his life?

Spanish countries. Spanish is widely spoken in large areas of the world. List the countries where Spanish is the main language. Ask a librarian or teacher to help you find this information. Locate some of these countries on a map. In many other countries, some people learn Spanish as a second language for their work.

Mystery country. The largest country in South America does not speak Spanish! Look at a map of South America and find the biggest country. What is its name? Now check this country's entry in an encyclopedia or an almanac to find out the main, or official, language. Where did this language originally come from? Do you think Spanish-speakers can understand it? What is the reason this country speaks another language?

MORE BOOKS TO READ

Brazil. Festivals of the World series. Susan McKay (Gareth Stevens)

A Child's Introduction to the Letters and Sounds of Spanish. Gwen Connelly (NTC Publishing Group)

Colombia in Pictures. (Lerner Group)

Columbus Day. Vicki Liestman (Lerner Group)

The Incas. Kathryn Hinds (Benchmark Books)

Mexico. Festivals of the World series. Elizabeth Berg (Gareth Stevens)

Peru. Festivals of the World series. Leslie Jermyn (Gareth Stevens)

Puerto Rico. Festivals of the World series. Erin Foley (Gareth Stevens)

VIDEOS

Beginning Spanish Language: I Can Read Spanish Signs, Pt. 1 & Pt. 2. (Video Knowledge)

Christopher Columbus. (Spoken Arts)

The Colombian Way of Life. (AIMS Media)

WEB SITES

www.nationalgeographic.com/resources/ngo/maps/atlas/samerica.html

www.nationalgeographic.com/resources/ngo/maps/atlas/namerica/namerica.html

Patricia Reilly Giff is the author of many fine books for children, including *The Kids of the Polk Street School* (series), *The Lincoln Lions Band* (series), *The Polka Dot Private Eye* (series), and *New Kids at the Polk Street School* (series). Ms. Giff received her bachelor's degree from Marymount College and a master's degree in history from St. John's University. She holds a Professional Diploma in Reading and a Doctorate of Humane Letters from Hofstra University. She was a teacher and reading consultant for many years. Ms. Giff lives in Weston, Connecticut.

DyAnne DiSalvo-Ryan has illustrated numerous books for children, including some she has written herself. She lives in Haddonfield, New Jersey.